I0709256

SWEET DELICIOUS CANDY

BY

JOHN WARD

Dark fiction drabbles

SWEET DELICIOUS CANDY

Edited by Kacey Flynn

Book design and layout by Vestan Pance

Cover image: Ministocker/Shutterstock.com

For more information and/or a place to send hate mail, please visit www .arbutusfilms.com

ISBN: 978-1-7383580-0-7

eISBN: 978-1-7383580-1-4

For Maggie and Oskar

Contents

1

The swarm

The SUV rocked as the dead clawed at the glass, their gnashing teeth mere inches from my flesh. Inside was dark, as the mass of bodies were so densely packed that sunlight itself couldn't break through. "Please, God," I muttered and tried the ignition again. My heart leapt briefly as the engine spluttered and caught. I hit the gas and punched a hole through the forest of limbs. Only it didn't last. It died, taking the dregs of my hope with it. I sank into the seat and stared at the lifeless eyes and ravenous mouths pressed against the windshield.

2

Calorie cutting

The mirror-figure spoke without words, but in his mind he heard its deafening voice proclaim he was fat. True, he had put on a few pounds over the pandemic, but he didn't feel out of shape – at least not until the voice urged him to look at himself. He looked on in horror as the reflected belly swelled before his eyes and dark laughter reverberated through his skull. There was only one way to silence it. He rushed into the kitchen and grabbed the carving knife. He'd shed those pounds as easily as he carved a joint of holiday ham.

3
Stuffed

He knew ecstasy: it was the warm sensation that arose from consuming a hearty meal. But that delirium left along with his lover leaving him hollow and unsatisfied. Determined to recapture that sensation he stuffed yet more pasta into his mouth. Sticky sweat oozed from every pore, and each laborious breath consumed more energy than the last, but he could taste ecstasy - a solitary tickle in the pleasure centre of his brain. Blinding pain tore through his belly. His thin gut lining erupted as the distended stomach exploded, exposing his inner workings. He collapsed, a smile on his lips.

4

Bad code

⁓

She draped herself over the toilet and vomited dark bile into the bowl. She had the virus. Her head pounded. Her guts were on fire. She fought the urge to purge but instead coughed up viscous black spittle that left a nasty metallic aftertaste. To her horror she noted the vile fluid comprised microscopic ones and zeros which disintegrated upon contact with the bowl water. What the fuck was that? Some kind of nano-fluid? If only she hadn't answered that call. If only she hadn't heard that dissonant machine noise. She heaved once more, spewing code all over the bathroom.

5

That's the way to do it!

☠ ☠ ☠ ☠

Did he hear something? Brian paused mid-swing and listened. There was no sound save for the gentle lapping of waves - and Punch's reedy whispers urging him on. He swung the hammer and smashed through a forest of matted hair, cracking the vagrant's skull like an egg. Punch was pleased. Brian sighed with relief, happy that his miserable life had purpose once again, and mildly embarrassed at how foolish he had been to try and throw it away. He may have started as the puppeteer but in the end he had come to realize he excelled at being the puppet.

6

Bit coin

I was skeptical about selling my little toe until I witnessed the bidding frenzy and then I eagerly volunteered to sell more of my useless vestigial structures. The little toe on my right foot went for double what the left made, but the floodgates opened before I could comprehend what was happening. One bidder purchased my foot, another took my leg. I waved to the auctioneer and lost my hand. I shouted and someone snapped up my larynx. I fainted as the ferocious crowd carved up the rest of my being – first with their tongues and finally with their blades.

7

Tails never fails

— 💀 — 💀

Tucking the pistol into her belt, she tossed the coin into the air. Before her the kneeling man breathed rapidly, his dark eyes barely visible under clumps of greasy hair. He wouldn't look at her. She needed to look into his eyes – only that way would she know if he was guilty. "Tails never fails," he said as she produced the coin. She hated leaving these decisions to chance but felt this time was different. The coin landed on the flat of her palm and she slapped it onto the back of her wrist to reveal its judgmental face. Heads.

8

Last will and testament

Holy shit you see that what the fuck no what are you doing let's get the fuck outta here you saw what happened to Bob oh no oh shit don't move its right there but I don't think it can see us no it can see us it's coming run no this way Alice trust me I know I said that before but I didn't know it was real I thought it was just a story Alice no oh God please get me outta this I said I was sorry please I'll do anything I don't wanna die I --

9

Bad hair day

~ ~

He stared at his reflection in the bathroom mirror and gingerly touched his unruly hair. Barely two hours ago he woke to find himself choking on his thick locks. His hair wanted him dead so he attacked it with the electric razor, cleaving it to the scalp. Now it was back. He knew this was his ex's doing, she had cursed him for cheating on her and he vowed to get even once he was done here. He bent over and dipped his head into the solution of lime and lye in the washbasin. There was acrid smoke. He screamed.

10

A letter to Santa

S anta,

As you continue to shirk all forms of communication I have little choice but to submit this request by letter. I grow weary of the ceaseless glut of gift requests arriving at my fortress and demand restitution. To mitigate ongoing confusion I request you cease and desist from using the name *"Santa"* in favour of a less similar moniker, preferably one that does not tip-toe up to the line of trademark infringement. Failure to comply with this request will be met with the deadliest of force or a visit from my lawyer - one R. Giuliani.

Frustratedly yours,

Satan

11

In from the cold

🕱 🕱 🕱

I peered out the window, heart pounding in my chest. The snowman was lifeless in the yard braving the early winter storm, and I began to feel silly for believing Amy Nicholls when she said it was coming for me. I was about to head downstairs when a strange sound caught my attention. I looked outside but now the yard was empty. My blood froze.

The howling wind blew open the front door. Instinctively, I reached for the door handle but couldn't bring myself to open it. I heard the strange slopping sound on the carpeted stairs outside my bedroom.

12
Rain, rain, go away

The downpour was heavy and savage and there was no hiding place. Those who were caught outdoors died horribly, their flesh slowly dissolving until they were nothing more than puddles of proteins. Those who made it to their vehicles thought they were safe, but the rain found them too, eating through the metal chassis like it was cotton candy. I watched it all unfold from the relative safety of my Teflon prison. They said I was delusional when I warned them about the storm. Some called me worse. I watched them all melt in the hot summer rain and smiled.

13
Into the deep

S he gasped as cold, dark water enveloped her. Her arms flailed. Her chest burned, and when she saw the heavy chain twisted around her legs, she wanted to scream. Azure became indigo as she descended. Strange, curious fish nibbled at her clothing. Her chest pain was now white hot. Her head felt heavy and ready to explode. Precious gas bubbles seeped from her pursed lips, and she wondered if she would lose consciousness. She looked up at the pinprick of distant sunlight. She tasted salty fluid and her lungs erupted in an effervescent froth. She surrendered herself to the white.

14

Musings on the purpose of life

T he large crow hopped onto my lifeless chest and cawed, signalling the nearby flock. They descended en masse, gouging the soft flesh of my corpse with razor-sharp bills and plucking my lifeless eyes from their sockets. I watched in impotent horror. My essence had found refuge in a nearby scarecrow after I was shot. I bellowed. I tried to move the flaccid straw limbs but the birds were unafraid. *Why*? The question gnawed at me as the fiends eviscerated my remains for it reflected a primal fear of my own. *What was a scarecrows purpose if not to scare crows*?

15

Treading water

Something sucked him into the sand. We locked eyes before he vanished, and in that horrible moment I knew something unspeakable was about to occur. A geyser of blood erupted from a silicon blowhole, showering us in gore. I dived into the tropical azure waters surrounding the lonely island paradise and watched as one-by-one the other tourists disappeared into the beach, their remains spat out in violent rouge fountains. I knew the boat wouldn't return until tomorrow but pushed the thought from my mind, along with the first twinges of cramp. Could I tread water until then? I hoped so.

16
Transmogrification

Flickers of moonlight stretched across the tumultuous sky, reaching for me as I rushed home. Creatures such as myself don't have the luxury of forgetting when the moon is full. Our cycles, indeed our very nature, are aligned with the ebb and flow of orbital mechanics. But the world has changed since I was reborn. Mindless distractions and subtle climate shifts have impacted my ability to sense the coming changes. I need to return before the transformation. It's the only way to ensure the safety of everything I love. Failure means I become a monster. Failure means I become human.

17

Killing horizon

"Come on." She leaned on the thrusters and the small ship shuddered violently. Although she couldn't see the event horizon she knew it was close, and that she was on the wrong side of its undetectable membrane. Crossing over had reversed the direction of space and time and she found herself endlessly circling back to the incident, reliving the explosive destruction of the large mothership again and again. She urged the shuttle forward but it was too late. The fuel was gone. Gravity had her now. She sank into her seat as the invisible horizon receded, and awaited the singularity.

18

Sweet, delicious candy

She could smell candy on the evening breeze. She closed her eyes and let the intoxicating perfume wash over her, rekindling memories of bygone nights filled with jack-o'-lanterns and costumes and excitement. The mouth-watering scent lured her to a bustling suburban street where the candy ran freely. Drunk with anticipation she sank her teeth into a discarded treat and gorged herself, savouring the sweet ichor as it exploded on her tongue. She retreated before the enraged man was upon her. Looking back as she fled, she saw him try vainly to stop the blood gushing from the child's severed artery.

19

White noise

"**S**hut up," he yelled and clasped clammy hands over his ears. The respite was only temporary as the static increased in both intensity and volume. Where it came from he didn't know, but its angry buzzing made his head hurt. He rushed into the second bedroom now masquerading as an office and threw on his noise-cancelling headphones. The pain vanished and for a brief moment there was relief – but then the static returned. His head throbbed as the pressure built rapidly; his arteries ruptured and blood spewed from eyes, ears and nose. He screamed and screamed until his head exploded.

20

Identity crisis

I don't know who I am. I gasped as the realization struck me and felt a rising panic in my gut. I spied a bright green rubber band wrapped around my wrist. My name was Greene. Timothy Allen Greene. The words resonated clearly in my mind but felt distant. I looked around the gym changing room and gasped in horror. Mutilated body parts littered the floor. The cold beige tiles were soaked with scarlet blood. What happened? Where am I? How did I get here? Why do I have a knife in my hand? I don't know who I am.

21

#NoFilter

Tania stared at the flipped image on her phone. There was something strange about the lighting. Resigned to yet another re-shoot, she pushed play and watched the video. Her stomach dropped as she watched the waif-like horror coalesce from the shadows, encircling her with freakish arms before slashing her throat. Tania gasped as her video-reflection spasmed; blood erupting from a severed artery. Shaken, she deleted the video and tossed her phone aside. She became aware of an unsettling change. The air around her grew thick with static. The shadows merged and the fiend took form. It looked just like her.

22

October people

When fall arrives you can always identify the summer people. They're the ones sipping PSL at the pumpkin patch, visiting the haunted house, wearing costumes to Halloween parties and performatively proclaiming that fall is their favourite season. October people - like me - smell the gentle perfume of death on the cool breeze and know what lurks in the darkness. You pass by us on the street but never see us – at least until it's too late. You beg for mercy and offer us rewards, but all we need is your blood and your soul; an offering to the darkness.

23
Haunting silence

Despite their promises, they had all left. She alone remained in the derelict mausoleum that had once teemed with life in all its messy forms. Then came the cataclysm, erasing all but inorganic matter. The others had crossed over but she could not. She knew no other existence. She had lived and died inside these bustling walls and feared what was beyond. Her powers waned as the silence grew more oppressive - until she was little more than a weakened husk; no longer haunting the minds and monuments of men, but cowering and fearful in the face of the haunting silence.

24

Black Friday

I never expected Hell to look like this. There were no fires. No demons. I was confused. Maybe I wasn't dead after all?! I was in a big box store dressed in a blue polo shirt and bland khakis. Other staff were lined up beside me, each dressed in the exact same outfit. I nodded to my neighbour but he turned away. An alarm sounded, so loud I felt the floor reverberate. An irate mob burst through the front doors, decimating every-thing in their path. As they trampled me underfoot, I spied a torn banner that read: Black Friday Sale.

25

An unusual delivery

The stench was truly obnoxious but Dave had no choice. He darted into the nearest cubicle and locked the door. Half the toilet seat was missing but his gut was overwhelming. He barely had time to drop his pants before it came. There was an explosive gushing and he thought he would pass out. Then it was over. Dave laughed but then felt warm rising liquid beneath him. He jumped as something unspeakable bubbled up the ceramic white bowl and poured itself onto the cracked tile floor. The unspeakable filth slithered into the restaurant to a chorus of terrified screams.

26

Pareidolia

— 💀 💀 — 💀

From afar the mountains looked truly majestic, but up close they were terrifying. Emma sensed the ancient power in the ionized air. She glanced at the steep, craggy rockface towering over them and saw the face staring back at her. She blinked, assuming it was an optical illusion, but a second glance proved her wrong. There was definitely a face. Two eyes. A nose and a mouth that moved as though aping speech. The car rounded a curve but the face somehow remained visible. *How was that possible?* Cacophonous thunder rolled towards them; an endless tsunami of ancient rock.

27

Survivor's Guilt

I hear her cultured yet deceitful voice every time I close my eyes. "Choose," she said. "You or your wife." I still feel the cold steel of the Luger pushing against my forehead. I fix on Hannah's terrified eyes across the room, their telepathic message failing to reach the listener in time. The words fall from my lips before I can stop them. "Shoot me."

If only it had been that simple.

I heard the loud crack of the pistol.

I saw Hannah silently collapse. Dead.

The demented laugher engulfed me, its latent echo forever trapping me in that cell.

28
Baby food

She placed a warm and unexpected hand on his thigh. He reciprocated with a smile.

"We have to be quick. I need to feed the baby." She pushed the stroller aside and dropped to her knees before him, grasping at his belt.

His groans morphed into inhuman squeals. He tried to push her away, but somehow she was latched onto him. Blood gushed from his orifices. His skin mottled then turned blue. He collapsed onto the bench, rigid as a Ken doll.

She stood and pulled the stroller to her then vomited the sticky residue into her offspring's hungry jaws.

29

Home To Roost

"The chickens are laying cucumbers again," screamed my Mom from the back yard.

I was skeptical when I first heard this story, but after hearing about the size and smell of the mini-cucumbers I was almost convinced. Almost. Of course, the eggs were perfectly regular but she vociferously insisted they were cucumbers. Her mental acuity had declined rapidly but she refused all help. "I'm fine," she'd argue. To my shame I didn't force the issue; not until I stopped in and found Dad with a knife in his chest.

"Coming mother." I picked up my axe and headed out back.

30

Dropped call

I could feel the agitated buzzing of my phone in my pocket but chose to ignore it. *If it was important they would call back.* But as the buzzing continued I pulled it from my pants; the act seemingly silencing the device. A cursory scan revealed there was no call - just a text message notification. It was my mother checking up on me. My spine tingled as I read her cheerfully obnoxious text message. Even though it was a warm summer evening, I swore I could see my breath condense before my eyes. She had been dead for years.

31

Error of judgment

The woman who opened the penthouse door wasn't the girl I grew up with. She had been timid and aimless while this woman was powerful, and her rags-to-riches narrative filled tabloid columns. Gripping - but untrue.

"I knew you'd come," she said.

I brandished my crucifix and pushed my way inside. "Demon. I order you to leave this host." I stabbed her with my concealed blade.

I knew the screams of fiends skewered by the holy metal. I was prepared for their desperate bargaining. But she collapsed, blood spurting from the rupture, her eyes wide with fear, her lips silent.

32

Date night

~ ~ ~

Hannah leaned back and sipped the merlot, a 2019 Joseph Phelps Insignia she had been saving for a special occasion. Across the table her oblivious and selfish husband shovelled blueberry cheesecake into his mouth, spewing crumbs and spittle in all directions. Shouldn't he be dead by now? She glanced at her uneaten dessert and her pulse quickened. Had she slipped up? Had he somehow switched plates? Why was he looking at her like that? Did he know?

There was a loud crash from the kitchen and her stomach dropped.

"Danny!" She rushed to assist her curious, and hungry young son.

33

Hard Time

"Stop!" The officer raised his hands and the mixer truck came to a stop mere feet from the hole carved into the damp-smelling earth.

The officer peered into the depths where the young woman lay in wait, one arm reaching into the drum of a front-loading washing machine. She grinned and waved back at him with her free hand, patiently awaiting her inevitable arrest.

"It's nothing," he yelled back to the driver. "Just an empty hole. Probably best to fill it in."

"Hey. I'm down here!"

The young woman's screams were drowned out by the raging torrent of quick-drying cement.

34

Day-walkers versus sleepwalkers

The thing you get wrong is that vampires *can* go out in daylight. Did you really believe reflected photons from the moon are different from those emitted by the sun? Of course you did. The lack of higher thinking is indicative of your species. You're too busy scouring the maze for strategically-placed cheese to realize you exist in order to be sacrificed to the great experiment. Isn't that the greater evil? You call us monsters. You relegate us to fable to preserve your notion of a rational universe. But in the end are you not the ones who fear illumination?

35

68 Seconds

bove me the plane banked and turned for home. My eyes never strayed from it even as I fell. The soldiers assumed I was still sedated when they tossed me out the cargo door, and since I'd been bound and gagged like a mummy there was little I could have done to alert them. I kept my eyes fixed on its fuselage, desperate to avoid looking down at my fast-approaching oblivion. I needed to know this wasn't all in vain.

The plane exploded in a blinding flash. My heart soared even as the unrelenting darkness of the ocean engulfed me.

36

Dead leg

The leg was grey and waxen from toes to groin. I gingerly touched the discoloured flesh and recoiled at the ice beneath my fingers. The leg was mine.

I awoke with a throbbing sensation in my calves, and found myself unable to kick off the bed-covers. As the dream-fog lifted I impatiently snatched the covers aside to reveal the strangely inactive limb.

I was paralyzed by questions. Who should I call? What would I tell them? Was this a virus? Was I infectious? The thought spurred me to examine my other leg. It was already gone, taken at the groin.

37

Permanent resident

The locals' stories had piqued her curiosity about the statue of the graveyard angel. She ignored their desperate pleas and soon found herself in its towering presence. While patches of moss and tendrils of ivy covered much of the neighbouring tombstones, the statue was strangely unmolested. It was clearly neo-classical in design but appeared to have been cut from ancient granite. Under its lifeless gaze her limbs became heavy. With rising panic she tried to flee but it was too late. The warnings of the locals rang in her ears, now more stone than flesh. Stay away or stay forever.

38
Hunger

I stared at my reflection in the mirror. There was a mouth just under my left armpit. Assuming it was dirt I tried to scrub it off only to receive a nasty bite from the sharp fangs lurking within its maw. To say I was stunned was an understatement. My arm felt and looked normal, except for the mouth that had sprouted overnight. It tore through the bandages I wrapped around it. It devoured a t-shirt, a sweater, and a jacket, growing larger with each snack. I wondered how much time I had before it would try to devour me.

39
Drained

He turned on the TV remote as he sank into his couch, hoping some mindless entertainment would dull the ceaseless headache. This late night ritual was practically the only pleasure he could derive after another punishing day as a wage slave, but even now he sensed fatigue getting the better of him.

He awoke with a disoriented jolt, absent-mindedly swatting away the fibrous tendrils that had sprouted from the couch. Startled, he tried to rise but felt resistance. With his fingertips he caressed the field of fattened filaments burrowing into his back. His mind screamed as tiredness again overcame him.

40
Circle of life

The initial excitement had soured and now all Marco felt was gnawing fear. He had dropped Chelsea off at maternity an hour ago but still hadn't found a parking spot. His pulse raced as he began yet another loop of the hospital campus. The sweat was thick on his palms, and the voice in his head was convinced he was going to miss the birth. Marco stopped in the middle of the lot. Parking spot or not, he had to get inside. His chest tightened. He felt exhausted. He needed to rest, unaware that this moment would became an eternity.

41

Lost and found

I easily evaded my pursuers. The dense foliage can be unforgiving to strangers, but to those who know its secrets it shall deliver salvation. I picked a handful of the red leaves that sustained me the first night and ate heartily. The cramps were terrible, but a worthy price to pay for their knowledge. I watched until the guards left and then returned to the watering hole to lap the warm fluid on all fours. Too late, I heard them. They grabbed me from behind, and spoke but their words lacked any meaning. Grandpa Tim? I don't know Grandpa Tim.

42

Twenty years

S ome nights are worse than others. If I'm lucky I'm still in bed when I wake. If I'm unlucky…

The dream repeatedly pulls from my memory. I look on as the thug punches my friend in the face and I turn away. It has haunted me for twenty years. They tell me my dreams are a healthy attempt to work through my sense of shame, but then I tried to set the nurse on fire while sleepwalking. Now they drug me and tell me I can no longer dream. I smile and nod, suppressing the desire to set them alight.

43

Brown note

Like most guitarists, Rollins continuously mocked my bass-playing. He belittled me in front of his musician friends, describing my sound as pedantic atonal dirge, and I often fantasized about maiming him. During our final rehearsal he stoked my anger to new levels. I pounded the strings, ripping my fingers to shreds and turning the fret board red. Each subsequent note made me queasy; my stomach knotted and churned as the guitar produced a slew of guttural tones. Across the room, Rollins screamed as blood poured from his eyes and mouth. I couldn't stop playing – not even when he finally exploded.

44

Know it all

"And I'll tell you something else—," he stopped mid-rant. The wasp had flown into his mouth and landed on the soft damp surface of his tongue and leisurely rubbed its forelegs, oblivious to the stress it caused. Liam breathed rapidly through his nose and opened his jaw as wide as it would go. I would've felt terrible if he wasn't a mouthy know-it-all.

Finally the wasp alighted, but at the last it stung him. Liam shrieked. He spluttered. His skin turned blue. The engorged tongue pushed against his pale lips.

The construction site was deserted. I left him there.

45

Mama's boy

His cracked lips latched to the dark areola; his flickering tongue caressed soft nipple tissue but the milk still wouldn't flow. He howled with disappointment as he lifted his jowls from the breast. He prodded the quivering flesh, hoping that would initiate the let-down, but he was to be disappointed. Dead women couldn't lactate. He felt a sensation in his gut, a dull ache that quickly became acute. He recognized it but couldn't put it into words. If his mother had only said yes... if only he hadn't given into the rage... but he was still a kid; only 23.

46
The cleansing

Peter groaned loudly as he let himself sink into the tub. He had never understood his wife's love of hot baths until this moment, but as he felt the warm and loving embrace of the immersive fluid all his aches and pains melted away. Below the surface he heard nothing but warm, comforting silence, interrupted by the distant echo of his own pulse. Unable to hold his breath he broke the surface and sat upright with a smile on his face. He cupped the bloody fluid and marveled at how long it remained warm after being drained from a body.

47

Becoming human

The blender sat patiently on the marble counter. Two human ears protruded from either side of its cylindrical bowl, the flesh and bone fused with the plastic. A single brown eyeball dangled from the end of a bloody thread of optic nerve, somehow spliced into the power cable. The machine heard the approaching footfalls and giddy laughter of the prospective home-owners. It quietly tested its rotary blades then fell silent as the couple entered the kitchen. The larger man stepped close, no doubt curious about the grotesque blender. Blades whirred. He screamed. The blender snarled with its newly acquired lips.

48

The pacifier

—

Alice needed sleep. She stared at the television and ignored the piercing screams coming from the bedroom. The doctor said there was nothing wrong with the baby, that it was colic and everything was normal. Alice knew better. Babies didn't scream like that unless something was wrong. Only the man on the television believed her. He listened, and counselled her with his warm and comforting voice. The baby was a demon and needed to be sent back to hell – only then would Alice be able to sleep. She picked up the butcher's knife. She needed rest, one way or another.

49

Wrong number?

- - -

Amanda cocked her head and listened for the faint, incessant ringing. She slipped into Stacy's bedroom, silently cursing Mark for giving her a cell-phone without permission and made a mental note to scold him when he returned her on Sunday evening. Amanda gingerly navigated the minefield of abandoned toys and threw open the closet door. The ancient Fisher Price rotary telephone sat there, ringing. She stared at it. Her brain rejecting what her senses could detect. Finally she snatched up the tiny blue receiver.

"Stacy ain't comin' home," the bass voice chortled in her ear.

Amanda let the receiver fall.

50

The procedure

I t was a simple tale about a hungry woman who went to the grocery store, yet the more he read it the more he sensed there was something deeper and more powerful going on. He knew the short, staccato sentences hid a subliminal message – not in the words on the page, but in the spaces between them and in the specific choices in vocabulary and syntax. He alone understood the text was an iceberg; that its true meaning lay hidden in the murky depths. He alone heard the distant voice guiding him to remove the brain tumour with the screwdriver.

Thanks

I couldn't have done this without the continuous love and support of Maggie and Oskar. I'm also indebted to the Johns family, Richard, Judy, and Katie, for being so welcoming and generous, and to my editor, Kacey Flynn, who helped elevate the stories and tried to correct my spelling.

This book wouldn't exist without the support of my incredible Kickstarter backers, in particular, Lawrence Denvir, Amanda Eschmeyer, Mary Jane Lloyd, Jillian Mon, and Sladist. Thank you for everything.

About the Author

JOHN WARD is a Vancouver-based writer, filmmaker, and podcaster. He's the creator and host of the 49 Degrees North Writers Podcast, has made award-winning short films such as Solus, and Linda, and several comic books including Acausal, Dark Fragments, and Scratcher. He is a graduate of the UCLA professional program in screenwriting and was previously a recipient of the Telefilm Canada New Voices Award. Before that John was a theoretical physicist holding a PhD in string theory from Queen Mary University of London, and worked at CERN, the University of Iceland, and the University of Victoria. He now lives on the West Coast where he enjoys kayaking, cooking curry, and spending time with his family.

Stay in touch

STAY IN TOUCH

Sign up for my monthly newsletter to receive updates, freebies, podcasts, and essays by scanning the QR code below or by visiting my website www.arbutusfilms.com. Let me know what you thought of the book!